JP
HAL

To Sam, our newest itty-bitty kitty baby
—S.H. & L.P.

The illustrations for this book were created entirely in Procreate.

Cataloging-in-Publication Data has been applied for and may be obtained from the Library of Congress.

ISBN 978-1-4197-5093-9

Printed and bound in China
10 9 8 7 6 5 4 3 2 1

Abrams Books for Young Readers are available at special discounts when purchased
in quantity for premiums and promotions as well as fundraising or educational use.
Special editions can also be created to specification. For details, contact
specialsales@abramsbooks.com or the address below.

Abrams® is a registered trademark of Harry N. Abrams, Inc.

ABRAMS The Art of Books
195 Broadway, New York, NY 10007
abramsbooks.com

PRETTY PERFECT KITTY-CORN

SHANNON HALE & LEUYEN PHAM

Abrams Books for Young Readers · New York

UNICORN is perfect.
Everybody thinks so.

"His horn is shiny; his coat is clean," says Gecko.

"His tail is as purple as a dream," says Parakeet.

Even his best **Kitty-CORN** friend thinks so.

"You're perfect!" says **Kitty**.

"Stay right there. I'm going to paint you."

UNiCORN holds as still as a marble statue. He yearns to look the way everyone thinks he should.

"He is simply resplendent from hooves to horn," says Parakeet.

"There's no one more perfect than Unicorn," says Gecko.

"Hmm, something is missing from my painting," says Kitty. "It just doesn't look right."

Not right? Is **UNiCORN** doing something wrong?

He lowers his magnificent haunches.
He stretches his neck long.
He reclines majestically.

Perhaps now he looks perfect.

"He's so flawless and so faultless that he's frankly sublime!" says Parakeet.

"My affection for his perfection makes it easy to rhyme," says Gecko.

"Something is still missing!"
says **Kitty**.

Oh no! UNiCORN stands and twists,
sways and spins, gallops in place, and
poses thoughtfully—all at the same time.

"That's it! It's perfect!"
exclaims **Kitty**.

Kitty adds a final
mark to her canvas.

"Come and behold my masterpiece!"

Gecko gapes. "What do I see?"
Parakeet gawks. "No, it can't be . . ."

But it is. **UNiCORN** must have sat in some paint. **UNiCORN** has a . . .

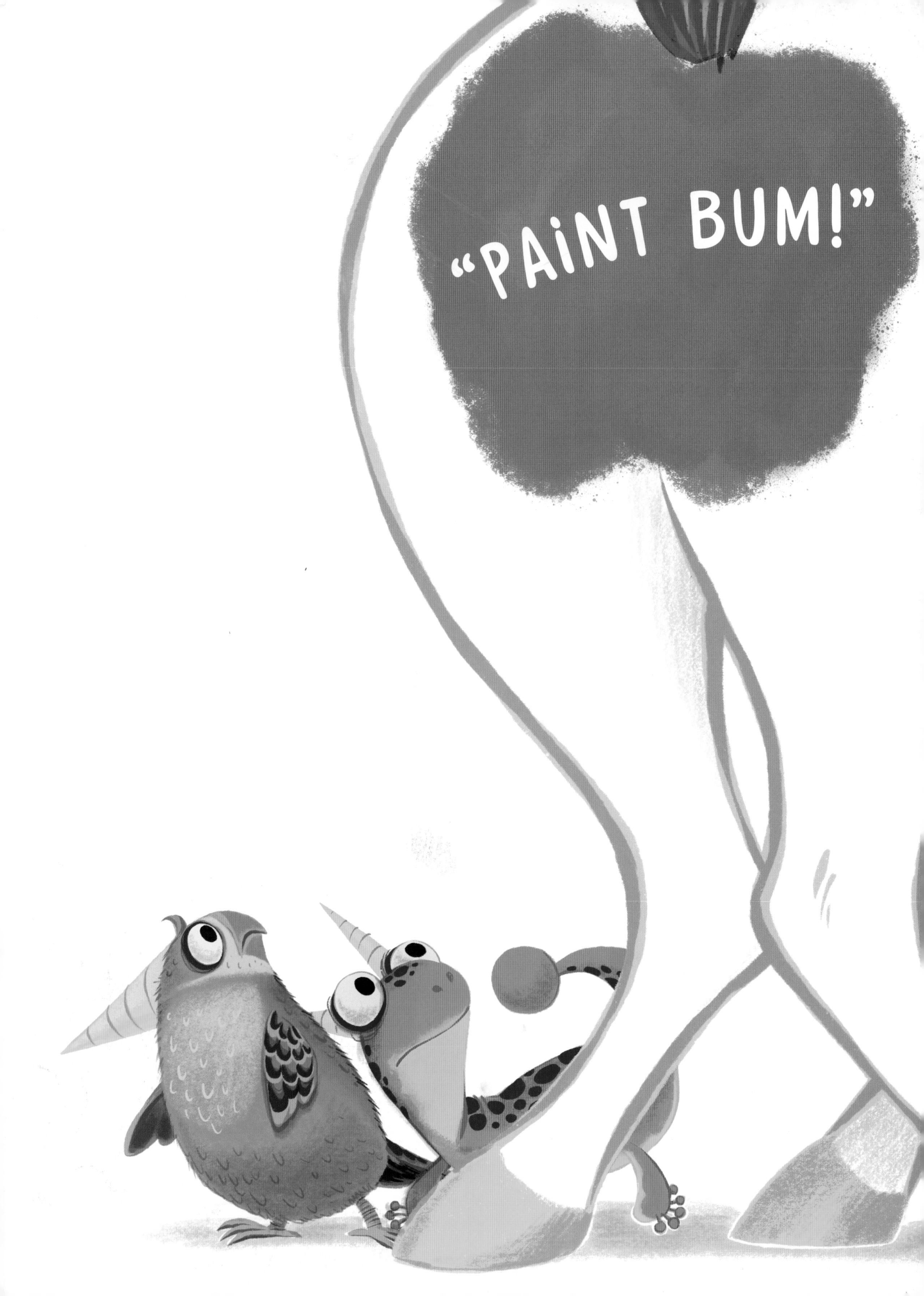
"PAINT BUM!"

"His mane is purple; his horn
is shiny," says Gecko.

"But there's paint all over
his huge white heinie!"
says Parakeet.

"UNiCORN?" asks Kitty.
"Are you OK?"

UNiCORN is not OK. Even the potted plant can't hide his shame. He feels like a big, ugly goof.

"Just ignore Gecko and
Parakeet," says **Kitty**.

"I don't care that they saw me with
a paint bum," says UNiCORN.

"Then why are you sad?"

"I care that *you* saw me
with a paint bum, Kitty."

"What?" asks Kitty, as shocked
as an eel. "ME? BUT WHY?"

UNiCORN doesn't know how to say it. How **Kitty** is the twin of his heart. How she is precious, like the last cookie.

And how he worries that, unless he's perfect, **Kitty** might not want to be his friend anymore.

But all he can say is "Because I just like you so much."

Kitty says, "I just like you so much too."

UNICORN is messy.

He has paint on his horn and the tips of his kitten ears. He has paint on his gold hooves and the ends of his tail. And he has a huge, glorious paint bum.

He'll definitely have a bath later. Warm and long, with plenty of bubbles to wash away the goop.

But for now, with **Kitty**, he can be messy.

With his best **Kitty CORN** friend, **UNiCORN** can be anything.